Praise for the Blood & Ancient Scrolls Series

"Meticulous worldbuilding, a dynamic protagonist, and plenty of blood."
— *Kirkus Reviews*

"You may come for the super sexy vampire action, but Blood Ex Libris will keep you entranced with its humor, dark violence, and smart storytelling."
— Amber Benson, *Death's Daughter*

"This delicious series has bewitched me. Raven Belasco has built a convincing, detailed world full of violence and romance."
— Patrick Califia, *Mortal Companion*

THE BLOOD & ANCIENT SCROLLS SERIES

Blood Ex Libris

Blood Demands

Blood Eternal

Blood Triad: Stories in the Blood & Ancient Scrolls series

Interview with the Vagabond King

Finding Bela Lugosi

ALSO

Adventures in Bodily Autonomy (Editor)

Serial Publication Font is used with permission by Kevin Christopher.

Library of Congress Cataloguing-in-Publication Data
Belasco, Raven.
That Lesbian Vampire Pirates Story / Raven Belasco
ISBN: 978-1-960942-17-3

1.Vampires—Fiction 2. US History—New York—1800s—Fiction 3. Lesbian—Fiction 4. Pirates—Fiction 5. Journeys—Journeys of personal growth—Fiction

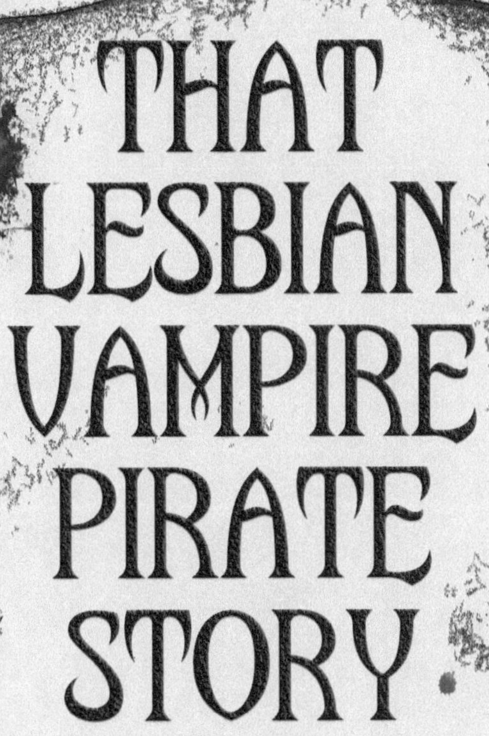

THAT
LESBIAN
VAMPIRE
PIRATE
STORY
A STORY IN THE
BLOOD & ANCIENT SCROLLS SERIES
RAVEN BELASCO

In Memoriam Cairngorm McWomble
the Terrible:
*Canis meus, terreus et ferox, semper
desiderari.*

And to Archibald Alastair McWomble:
my new co-writer, my brave heart, my
joy-bringer, my surprisingly sweet rescue(r)

"I want to talk about being a criminal because that's the only thing that makes sense to me now." — Kathy Acker, *Pussy, King of the Pirates*

"Coves, let us frog and toe!' ("Guys, let's go to New York!") — George W. Matsell, *Vocabulum; Or, The Rogue's Lexicon*

CONTENTS

Author's Note on Language

This book has a bunch of words and phrases that are not in English, or are archaic English from the 1860s. Some words are in the am'r language. The am'r words are given definition when they are first used, but if you forget any of them, there is a glossary in the back of the book.

There is an index of all the non-English and archaic words and phrases you will encounter along the way. If the meaning of those words is vital to the understanding of the story, I've made sure they get explained in the text, but feel free to flip to the back if you want to know the precise definition.

That Lesbian Vampire Pirates Story

When Sadie the Goat went to the Hole-in-the-Wall that night, it wasn't that she was going there to pick a fight with Gallus Mag. But if it just happened, well, she wasn't going to turn down the opportunity either.

She had been drinking in Sue the Turtle's bar. Big Sue ran a bordello above it, so she did have to stave off the occasional john who mistook her for a dell, but she liked Big Sue and Big Sue liked her, so her beer cost the "friend-and-family rate." And nobody minded if Sadie had stolen her beer money in the surrounding streets; not one other person in the bar had come by their earnings honestly either.

Sadie wasn't drunk. Just feeling *fine*. Feeling fine enough to whistle and skip a few dance steps as she wandered the byways of the Fourth Ward, which she knew like the veins on the back of her hand.

No one was going to bother this petite young miss, dressed as artfully as some careful trades of stolen goods for fine clothing with Marm Mandelbaum would allow. All Marm Mandelbaum's pretty garments were stolen too, of course. Sadie's trades had facilitated the flow of contraband stolen goods. Once items had been sold, they weren't "stolen" anymore, just "bought," made all above-board and shiny-legal again by the transaction.

No, no one would harass this girl who seemed too delicately pretty for her drab, desolate, degraded surroundings. The streets were ankle-deep in filth: dog shit, pig shit, cow shit, human shit, and the varied flotsam and jetsam of fifty families stuffed cheek-to-jowl in apartments built for four families, all throwing their filth out the nearest window. The decrepit buildings on either side would, in their disintegration, dump bricks on the heads of unwary passersby. You had to watch your feet and watch the skies and watch your pockets, walking the Fourth Ward.

But Sadie didn't need to pay quite as much attention, not unless she was looking for a mark. Everyone knew Sadie the Goat. Few men were left who were dumb enough to mess with her; enough of their number had made that mistake or been bystanders to when Sadie had found a mark ripe for plucking, and done her infamous maneuver upon him, leaving him gasping for air, on his back in the filth of the street, helpless against her sturdy boots and quick knife.

Sadie danced forward a little more and discovered herself at the corner of Water and Dover Streets. Her feet had led her to the Hole-in-the-Wall bar. And why not? She was starting to feel a thirst upon her again. She stepped quickly into the nearest alley and pissed the old beer away. She laughed as a rat was caught in the stream of hot urine and angled her hips to keep it in the spray as it tried to get away. Tonight, she was having fun.

As she skipped her way to the door of the Hole-in-the-Wall, it opened, and an imposing, stocky shape blocked her, filling the doorway like a secondary door of muscle and attitude. Sadie sighed. Gallus Mag. "Gallus" for the braces that held up her trousers, "gallus" for her brash manner and insolent approach to every aspect of life. Including interpersonal interactions.

Gallus Mag made a show of looking Sadie up and down with an offensive sweep of her eyes. Mag's dark blonde hair was in a short, choppy cut, greased back to keep out of her eyes. Those impertinent eyes were hazel-ish, not any particular color, just *angry* from the moment they opened in the morning to when they closed for sleep—if the suspicious mind behind them even allowed such an extravagance.

Then Gallus Mag stuck her thumbs into her suspender straps, leaned cheekily on the door frame, and said, "Well, if it ain't Mizz Sadie. You come here to stick your head where it don't belong, Goat-lady?"

"I *belong* here much as anybody, Gallus Mag. I'm a paying customer, same as the next hoody-doody come here for your rag-water. So, get out my way and stop playing the goosecap."

"If any person here is a goosecap, it's your own fine self, thinking I'll be letting you in here with our good fellows."

" 'Good fellows'—ha! Sharps and rogues the lot! But see here—what d'you have 'gainst me, Gallus Mag? I ain't done nothing for you to treat me like that."

"I'm the one what says who comes and who goes, that's what. And tonight, I *says* that you *goes*. So, mizzle, you dirty mab."

"You bottle-headed slubber! Shut yer gob and get out my way!"

Sadie pulled back a few steps, and went to do her signature move. But she hadn't used it on a woman before. She'd cut a purse from many a moll's skirts, but never actually fought one since the squabbles of childhood.

Fighting a woman was different than fighting a man, especially if that woman was built even more solidly than most men were. Mag was not impressed with Sadie's plan to head-butt her in the solar plexus. It was like she could anticipate all of Sadie's moves. Not that there were many. Sadie ran at Mag, and Mag simply grabbed Sadie by the braids coiled on her head and brutally yanked back. Sadie flailed with all the strength in her arms and legs, but Mag pinned her thrashing limbs, and leaned in, teeth bared. Instead of the loverly kiss it looked like she'd bestow, Mag opened her mouth wide and caught Sadie's ear. Then Mag pulled her own signature move, and bit with a paroxysm of strength. Sadie was suddenly experiencing more pain than she'd ever felt, in a life of pains widely varied in strength and kind. She dropped limply from Mag's arms. Her left ear did not accompa-

ny her. Gallus Mag spat it out in a dramatic spray of blood and held it up in the air,
crowing.

"Another for me jar! First ear off a bludget!"

The crowd—which hadn't been there
before the fight began but was now
packed 'round like they'd never *not* been
there—cheered the delicate light-brown
shell pinched between Gallus Mag's strong
fingers.

Sadie felt the *throb-throb-throb* of bleeding from where her ear had been. She
clasped her hand to the side of her head.
She was dizzy and confused. Everything had
been going so well. Then that oversized
catamaran had refused to follow along with
Sadie's plan, which was to knock her down,
give her some good kicks and a punch in
the ogles to remember Sadie by, and then
Sadie would be crowned the new Queen of

the Ward and might even get a drink on the house.

But none of that had happened. And now Sadie was sitting in the filth, pain screaming through her from where her ear had been, and, worst of all, the maddening crowd was jeering and mocking her: all had seen her defeat and humiliation. Her face screwed up, trying to keep her feelings from running down her cheeks.

But Mag noticed. "The mort is mouthin'!" she taunted. "Pike off home and snivel, leave the mill to real roughs, not *little girls*."

Sadie wanted to yell at her and attack her again. But her legs weren't working right, and her brains weren't either. It was all she could do to stumble to her feet and lurch away, trying to hold her hand tight enough to her head to keep the blood from running down her neck.

Heckles and abuse followed her until she stumbled around a corner and was able to lean against a wall and catch her breath. She let herself succumb to self-pity, but it was only because the beer had worn off and she never liked feeling sober very much.

She'd been accustomed to being one of the gentry of the Fourth Ward. People called out her name as she passed by, doffed a hat, complimented her dress or her hair; they wanted others to know *they* knew her. And those who didn't know her, well, if they tried anything, they knew her well enough in short order.

She'd been getting by on the element of surprise, she realized, a new rush of anger pumping hot through her. No one expected much of a slender, pretty girl. They certainly didn't expect her to fight back. Much less to *start* the fight—and *finish* it. But the fight with Gallus Mag tonight had shown her. Not what Mag thought it had shown her: that Mag was the rightful winner. No, it showed her she'd been getting lazy, had stopped staying one step ahead. On the streets of one of New York City's most infamous districts, the rule was "Stay Ahead of Every Other Fucker—Or Die."

The ear was a wake-up call. She hadn't died, simply donated an ear to Gallus Mag's famous jar of pickled ears. Some of New York's most feared bruisers had strutted up to the door Gallus Mag guarded, and hobbled away, just the same way Sadie had. Gallus Mag was more than a big woman; she was fueled with all the anger of an Irish immigrant forced to flee unendurable conditions where her countrymen starved to death in the streets, to find herself here in the slums of the biggest, most uncaring city, left to somehow survive unendurable indignities and privations until a plague took her or until she was caught by a surprise knife in the back. Add to that the burning anger of a woman unvalued by society, seen as good only for providing menial labor to her betters, not worthy of love or even encouraged to have a home and family.

Sadie, with her mixed blood that had made her skin a shade too dark to pass and her hair too coily (unless she could force it with a hot iron to be smooth and straight as "beauty" required) understood that anger well enough. She had come up North hoping to find better treatment, only to discover that racial hatred here was simply different, not *less*. In New Orleans she had a place in society as a *gens de couleur libre*, a woman who could wear a beautiful dress to a Quadroon Ball and find a rich white husband, or rise to prominence running a house in Storyville. But she had read about the Abolitionists in the North, and had, in youthful folly, made the mistake of thinking the majority of people Up North felt that way.

So far, she had not met *any* Abolitionists at all. If they existed, they were not in New York. At least not the parts of New York she had access to.

Sadie wasn't going to run away to anywhere, not back to New Orleans, not even back to the pile of rags (in a corner of a room in the overcrowded tenement) that was her "bed." And so she set off walking, to find out where it was she was going *to*.

She turned left onto Beekman Street, and at the end of it found herself at the piers. She ambled along, gazing down each dock at the ships and boats bobbing against their ropes.

Most of the vessels were quiet for the night, the sailors off getting lushy in the myriad bars and bordellos of the Fourth Ward.

After the main docks, she found a small-er landing, the timbers of it decrepit, barely still standing. It would soon enough be replaced with a big new pier, but for now it served to tie up a selection of unimpressive rowboats. And it was the one dock where there was action and life.

None of the men carried torches, but the moon was near full, and the light reflected off the water, so if your eyes were acclimated, you saw pretty well. And what Sadie saw were three rowboats trying to get outward-bound, but instead just presenting a comedic show as three men fought for "command."

"Slipsy, Piggy, and Suds, yar wit' me!"

"Naw, I gots Slipsy. Take Tommy."

"Tommy, ya goes wit' Saul. Slipsy, yar wit' me and Patsy and Pete."

"Big Bill, ya can't have Slipsy; I called him first!"

"Ya bottle-headed slubber—if I wants him I gots him. Take Scotchy and Wreck."

"Who ya callin' a slubber, ya nocky blunderbuss!"

"Shut yer potato-trap and give the red rag a holiday!"

The men looked to be near blows—if you could call them "men." Most were still on the boy side, scrawny and awkward-limbed, faces patchy with uneven hair and acne. The most impressive was the aptly-named Big Bill, who stood a head over all of them, and whose dark skin made him look like a dangerous shadow in the moonlight.

She knew the other ostensible leaders from around the way. Saul was a wiry little fellow with dark hair that grew to his shoulders in greasy waves. Razor Charley was older than the rest, a lawbreaking jack-of-all-trades by land, so she had no surprise he was trying out a wetter criminality as well.

She'd heard about the Charlton Street Gang, which is what this unprepossessing group had loftily appointed themselves. They'd committed some minor mayhem in the Hudson River, enough to make them swagger when back on land.

In that moment, Sadie knew with blazing clarity just where she was going. She straightened her skirts, adjusted her jacket and blouse collar, and reached up to touch her hair and make sure the poor abused braids were still coiled in their proper shape. She bit her lips to bring up the color and pinched her cheeks. Then she kicked out with her calf-length boot and strutted down the rickety landing, making sure not to trip on a nail or in a hole, but trip lightly *over* it all.

"You kinchin coves ain't getting nowhere fast," she informed them loftily, as they all turned to look at the sound of heels on rotten wood. "You need a sterner hand at the tiller, you looby ralphs."

"And might you know this sterner hand, Madam?" Razor Charley, being the oldest and most experienced, took up the challenge.

"It just so happens that I do, Razor Charley."

"Hey! It's Sadie th' Goat!" one of the boys cried.

"Why, thank you..." Sadie took a careful guess, "...Suds."

Suds blushed so red that it could be seen in the moonlight and elbowed the boy closest to him. "Hey! She got me down fine!"

"And will you be telling us who's to be our new captain, Miss Sadie?" Razor Charley was grinning, enjoying the game.

"Why Razor Charley, you're looking right at *her*."

They all stared for a speechless moment. They were not expecting *that*.

"Doff your hats to your Captain," she continued. "And I will sail with Big Bill and his boys. For tonight, that's the lead ark in this convoy."

While they were trying to wrap their heads around that, she reached out to Big Bill, and he handed her down into the front of the rowboat. The boys already in the boat (Slipsy, Piggy, and the still-beaming Suds) awkwardly doffed their hats.

"Hey, why ain't *my* ark the lead ark?" Razor Charley wanted to know. And that was how she got her foot in the door. Big Bill would back her now, and the boys on her "ark" would jealously insist on being her crew.

"You'll be the lead ship tomorrow night," she told Razor Charley. "Pirates is democratized. We ain't like the navy or nothing like that. Pirates got rights. They got a code, the Pirate Code. We follow that."

Young Sadie had been a voracious reader. Her father had been a very well-to-do gentleman, who had an unusually large library. Sadie's mother had the barest learning of readin'-n-'ritin', but what she taught her daughter gave Sadie the key to myriad worlds of fantasy and adventure. Sadie had been drawn to swashbuckling tales after finding *Pirates: The Lives and Adventures of Sundry Notorious Pirates* on the shelf. As soon as she finished that, she took up *The History of the Pirates: Containing the Lives of Those*

Noted Pirate Captains, Misson, Bowen, Kidd, Tew, Halsey, White, Condent, Bellamy, Fly, Howard, Lewis, Cornelius, Williams, Burgess, North, and Their Several Crews ... To which is added, a correct account of the late piracies committed in the West Indies; and the expedition of Com. Porter. Seeing the young girl poring through those books gave her father an excuse to order *Thrilling Narratives of Mutiny, Murder and Piracy: A Weird Series of Tales of Shipwreck and Disaster, From The Earliest Part of The Century To The Present Time, With Accounts of Providential Escapes and Heart-Rending Fatalities.*

While Sadie's mother attended to the Lady of the House—her father's wife—Sadie was allowed to read and to play games of pirates (and cowboys and knights in shining armor) with her father's other children. Her father treated her indulgent-ly, and almost always allowed her in the library. That all changed when Sadie's mother died. Sadie was twelve, and her father made it clear that Sadie would now be expected to keep his bed warm in her mother's place. That was when Sadie decided to gather her worldly goods and go North where the Abolitionists were.

So, Sadie knew about the Pirates Code and a pirate's life. All she had to do was teach these ackruffs how to be proper buccaneers.

The first night out, she sent her would-be-pirates onto boats of a similar size. There were plenty of smaller vessels in the waters around New York, both honest fishermen and less decent, law-abiding mariners. Fishermen made a good start, because growing boys are hungry.

So, some fishermen and their families went hungry while the Charlton Street Gang practiced boarding boats with unwilling boat-owners who were ready to put up a certain amount of fight with makeshift weapons. Since the Charlton Street Gang always outnumbered the fishermen, it was a guaranteed success, which is what all uncertain buccaneers need to grow bold.

Back at the gin mill at the end of Charlton Street, Sadie boiled fish and fried fish and grilled fish, seasoned not only with the spices of her childhood but the sweet taste of successful thievery. She fed her boys, along with warm praise, stinging critiques, the putting of any rash egos back into their place, and a supportive shoulder and ear for each hard story they had to tell, and soon they were eating more than fish out of her hands.

She couldn't believe she'd been content for so long to just be little Sadie the Goat, just one woman alone on the streets of the Fourth Ward. Running a pirate gang was so much finer, so much more *her*.

She couldn't quite thank Gallus Mag for being pushed out of her old life; her missing ear still throbbed with pain sometimes. As much as she wanted to change her hairstyles to cover the loss, she forced herself to change them to *emphasize* it, both as a lesson to never be forgotten, and also as a badge of rough boasting: *If I lost an ear and it didn't stop me, then* you *won't be stopping me, either!*

Before long, she had them move up to more perilous prey: other sea-going members of the criminal classes. There were three reasons for this: the first was that her boys might know how to scrap, but they needed to work on their sea-legged fighting skills; secondly that there would be no trouble with the law if they kept their activities within that particular sphere; and thirdly, eventually everyone would get tired of fish dinners.

This had gone predictably. At least as Sadie had predicted. Injuries were drastically increased, but mostly because her boys were still so lubberly about fighting on a rolling, sometimes bucking surface. But they were fighting exactly the men they knew how to fight, who had learned their pugilism in the same rough schools. Night after night, they came up against the Swamp Angels, the Short Tails, the Border Gang, and the Hockers— but they were all small fish, and none had more violence or sheer greed-driven determination than the Charlton Street Gang.

Except the Daybreak Boys. Their reputation for thievery, mayhem, and cold-blooded murder was not mere words, but hard-earned and maintained. In the years they had been run by Nick Saul and Billie Howlett, they had repossessed hundreds of thousands of dollars of goods, and "settled" more than fifty people. Sadie had been given on good authority that the requirement to join the Daybreak Boys was to kill someone of their choosing.

The only requirement to join the Charlton Street Gang was a willingness to put up with the other members of the Charlton Street Gang, which made it not quite as selective (or impressive) as the Daybreak Boys but was almost as much a barrier to entry.

Not that she didn't love them all in her way, but they did not wash frequently enough to suit her, and there were points where they all passed so much gas (something not one of them ever failed to find hysterically funny) that she had to step out onto the rickety roof of the gin mill to breathe the slightly less poisoned air of the Fourth Ward.

But today had been a red-letter day for the Charlton Street Gang. They had liberated from the Swamp Angels a couple more sturdy skiffs that were in a lesser threat of sinking during piratical activities (those who had been in the vessels had had to swim back to shore, with comments like "Good thing a Swamp Angel knows how t' dogpaddle!" being shouted after them.)

These skiffs were a small step to greater things. The true goal: the *Lucky Lish*, a beautiful sloop, her single forward mast gaff-rigged. She raced cleanly over the Hudson, barely conceding the choppy waters. The Daybreak Boys had originally liberated her from a would-be pleasure sailor who was more optimistic than realistic, and Sadie couldn't wait to liberate her further.

Sadie was enamored of her clean lines and most of all, of her *potential*. The *Lucky Lish* was the next stage towards what Sadie truly coveted. While small boats were good for mobbing a larger ship and making un-expected (and intensely unwanted) board-ings, Sadie wanted to be a proper pirate, putting fear in the hearts of all who saw her sailing a formidable ship with a Jolly Roger flapping ominously in the breeze from the mainsail, her equally terrifying crew jump-ing immediately (and preferably *efficiently*) to her every command.

With the *Lucky Lish*, Sadie could swift-ly and silently overtake any vessel dealing with the crowded ports of New York. She could carry more men, and once they had subdued their victim, the *Lucky Lish* could carry away far more *booty*.

Sadie wanted all of that. She wanted success and she wanted it in the form of victories that would spread by word of mouth, and in the form of money and goods which could be turned into money, because money was just as important as gossip to demonstrating and growing success. If she could afford the best clothing, and to move amongst a better class of society (not the respectable classes, yet, but a higher class of criminals), if she could afford to turn out her men better both in presentation and with better weapons, that would get her the most priceless jewel of all—respect.

There would be no more jokes about her ear still floating in a pickle jar back in the Hole-in-the-Wall, if she could layer on sufficient deference. No one would dare comment on her skin tone or hair texture if they feared her enough.

The way to that triumphant future was through the Daybreak Boys.

The *Lucky Lish* was clinging tight against the side of the battered old Hudson River sloop *Bierarsch*, loaded so heavily she sat dangerously low in the water. The *Bierarsch's* crew were putting up a valiant effort against the Daybreak Boys who had boarded them, but while the ship's crew desperately did not want to lose the valuable goods weighing the ship deeply into the sludgy waters of the Hudson, the Daybreak Boys were fighting with even more desperation on their side.

Back in the 1850s, the Daybreak Boys had been the most feared riverine gang in the city, led by Nicholas Saul and William Howlett. But after an act of piracy gone disastrously wrong, Saul and Howlett were hung by the neck until they were dead, dead, dead, and hundreds of New Yorkers turned out for the execution. Sow Madden and Slobbery Jim stepped up to take their place, but it was hard to keep up the untouchable reputation of the Daybreak Boys after watching their once-feared leaders soil themselves as they dropped. Not for lack of trying, the gang had still not been able to maintain the intimidation they once had held over the ports of New York.

This was Sadie's perfect opportunity to raise the Charlton Street Gang up to take the Daybreak Boys' place of preeminence in the underworld. And today was the day.

The two skiffs slid smoothly out from the shadows of a neighboring pier. It was no trouble to pull up fore and aft against the *Lucky Lish*, as the one man left in the boat was staring upwards at the battle, not doing his one job as lookout.

He was dead the instant Slipsy gently stepped over into the *Lish* and hit him over the head with a cosh as he began to turn around. He and Saul, Razor Charley, Scotchy, and Pete clambered up onto the deck of the *Bierarsch*, and Sadie, Big Bill, Suds, Patsy, and Wreck climbed into the stern— Tommy and Piggy were left miserable in the skiffs to *actually* be lookouts. Both groups immediately joining the fight on the *Bierarsch* crew's side, going at it with the Daybreak Boys with a superior desperation: that of upwardly mobile determination.

The Daybreak boys had more pistols—only Sadie and Saul held the two the Charlton Street Gang currently possessed—but they were not getting much chance to shoot them, as Sadie's boys were enthusiastically swinging about sticks that had formerly been brooms and shovels, liberally decorated with nails at the hitting end.

Sadie found herself holding her pistol out at Slobbery Jim, who was holding his out at her.

"What the fuck do yuh think yuh playin' at, missy? D'yuh know who we are?"

"You're Slobbery Jim. And no one cares anymore. The Daybreak Boys are over. So, this is your one chance to lay down your weapons and get out of this alive."

Slobbery Jim laughed so hard his pistol wobbled. Sadie's did not. "Yer fucking joking...is that you, Sadie the Goat? I thought I heard yuh'd taken up with the Charlton bens. But this takes the cake. Look, sweetheart, if you wanted my attention, you could have just met me at the Bunch o' Grapes; I drink there regular. I might even have stood you a tot! Put the gun down, be a bene blowen, and I'll show you what a *goat* I am—after I give these coves their consolation."

Slobbery Jim waved his gun-holding hand to indicate the Charlton Street Gang, fully to grips with the other Daybreak Boys. Sadie pulled the trigger and watched the impact: first the bullet hitting Slobbery Jim in the chest, and then the surprise on his face. He so slowly realized she'd shot him; the pain in his heart was a joy in hers.

Slobbery Jim dropped backwards, overboard into the Hudson. "I hate being underestimated," Sadie told him conversationally as he fell.

She turned her attention to the rest of the fighting. She had five more cylinders loaded with powder, wads, bullets, and caps, so her shots needed to count; not only would it take far too long to reload the gun, but the

Charlton Street Gang had used up all their ammunition loading the two revolvers they possessed.

There was not a large amount of space on the *Bierarsch*. Between the *Bierarsch's* crew, the Daybreak Boys, and now the Charlton Street Gang, people were packed like sardines on the crowded deck, and fighting was definitely hand-to-hand. Sadie's boys had tossed back the long sticks with nailed ends (which had been quite useful during the initial surprise of boarding, definitely worth the time it had taken to prepare them for this operation) back onto the skiffs and were going at the Daybreak Boys with knives and coshes and all their preferred close-fighting weapons.

There were already quite a few bodies down on the deck, not to rise again soon—or ever. This added to the chaos of the skirmish, as her boys were as likely to trip over a body as to take a hit.

"Scotchy! Pete! Suds! Wreck! Grab bodies and toss 'em overboard! Razor, Scotchy, Patsy: cover 'em!" Her shouting brought her back to the attention of the nearest Daybreak Boy, who had been still gaping at where Slobbery Jim had dropped from the boat, and from life itself.

"Yuh killed Slobbery Jim!" he screeched and lunged for her.

He was perhaps not used to women holding—and being entirely ready to use—guns. Her second shot hit his shoulder and spun him around in complete surprise. Big Bill had clambered over bodies and barrels and jumped down on him from a trunk, breaking his neck in the process. Bill tossed the body over the side with negligent ease.

"You bene, skipper?"

"Thank ya, Bill, that was very timely. Let's wind up this job 'n cap our lucky."

"Right, Cap'n!"

Big Bill climbed back to take on a Daybreak Boy who was trying to prevent Suds from tossing a not-fully-deceased Daybreak Boy into the Hudson. Sadie rotated with her pistol half-raised, looking for the next Daybreak Boy to shoot. But the crew of the *Bierarsch* had figured out what was going on and was now helping the Charlton Street Gang to dispose of Daybreak Boys. The Daybreak Boys who were not already dead or deeply wounded were jumping over the sides and swimming away from a lost cause. What was needed from Sadie now was words, not bullets.

She found an area on the deck where she could best be seen by all, despite the mainsail, and raised her voice authoritatively. "Crewmen of the *Bierarsch!* We're the Charlton Street Gang, and today we helped ya not be cramped by the Daybreak Boys. We ask only half yer cargo in repayment. Which is a square deal, ya must admit. So, if ya'll assist my lads in loading the *Lucky Lish* there with our chosen items, ya can sail off with yer lives and half yer cargo intact."

"And what if we do not help you?" asked a man she assumed was the captain. He was a heavily bearded old man in a wool sweater, weathered skin burnt dark from a sailor's life. He held his right arm at a bad angle, and blood was seeping through the wool of the sleeve. She had no doubt of his courage, so she had to come at him with reason, not threat. Or, just enough threat to make him see reason.

"Well, Captain, ya can see all around the evidence of what millin' coves my roughs can be. Yerself and many of your crew are injured already. It's in yer own best interest to keep yer lives, your ark, and half yer cargo, is it not? Is that not the best result ya can hope for, considering that my men are already on-board yer vessel and ready to hush yer culls? Ya can end this day with far less loss than ya expected not half an hour ago. Let us make this easy for ya."

"Ha! *Easy for me*, she says! As if the company will not be docking my wages for losing half these goods? *Na dann…*" The captain of the *Bierarsch* looked around at his crew, who were clearly eager to stop fighting and help these pirates off the ship, even if they took the whole cargo.

"*Verdammt*," he growled. "Take half then, and may it bring you no good thing." The captain stomped off to attend to one of his crew who was bleeding profusely upon the deck.

Sadie went around with Saul and Big Bill, checking the barrels and trunks. They were in great luck; the *Bierarsch* was carrying flour and spices, very valuable goods indeed, and no wonder the captain was in a foul temper. Sadie instructed Saul and Big Bill to take the spices first, and finish filling the rest of the *Lucky Lish* and the skiffs with the flour barrels after they had ensured they had the most valuable merchandise.

They worked fast. Sow Madden, the other current leader of the Daybreak Boys, had not been working this job, and the surviving members of the gang were no doubt running—*swimming*—as fast as they could back to tell him all about it.

While they didn't need Sow charging into an attack while they were sailing home laden heavily with their rich booty and pulling the two skiffs behind, once the goods had been offloaded with Marm Mandelbaum (who specialized in stolen textiles but who could reliably find a buyer for *anything*), Sow Madden and the remaining Daybreak Boys were a problem for another day. She had the *Lucky Lish* and as much as she needed to stay alert, the glory of this rushed intoxicatingly through her veins. This sweet sloop was what they had needed to start taking the bigger ships bringing far greater imports into the Port of New York.

She already had a Jolly Roger flag sewn. She hadn't dared bring it with her, for fear of jinxing today's enterprise, but as soon as the *Lucky Lish* was tied up in a safe mooring, Sadie would attach the dread flag to the topmast, and from now on, when the good citizens of New York saw her sailing the waters of New York, they would know a *real* pirate was amongst them, one to be seriously feared and admired. Soon, no one would remember that Gallus Mag—that *nobody*—had ever bested her. All they would know was that Sadie the Pirate and her crew of Dangerous Men were the true power in the New York underworld.

CHARLTON STREET GANG OUTRAGES THE HUDSON

◆

"THE SHIPPING AND COMMERCE OF OUR CITY IS THREATENED BY THESE VILLAINS" SAYS MAJOR TWEED

◆

AN ACCOUNT OF THE MOST EXTRAORDINARY CIRCUMSTANCES THAT HAVE BEEN TAKING PLACE ALONG THE HUDSON RIVER AND OTHER WATERFRONTS OF OUR CITY.

Last Friday the Charlton Street Gang struck again, this time boarding several shipping vessels and a private yacht in the course of one villainous night. The Victims all agree that the Gang is now led by A Woman Pirate, called by the Locals, Sadie The Goat. This Unnatural Woman is the Worst of the Criminals, and has in her Cruelty forced the Crew of more than one ship to Walk The Plank. This Murderess used to be merely a Violent Thief in the Fourth Ward, but Unknown Circumstances have led to her commanding this Vicious Pirate Gang as they Terrorize the Waterfront. All around the Upper Bay from the East River to the Hudson, no Honest Mariner or Merchant is safe from their Nocturnal Villanies. "We will not rest until we apprehend these Bloodthirsty Criminals who are disturbing the Trade and Commerce of Our City," says Sheriff Kell

Sadie sat in the prow of the good ship *Mary-Joan*—now *her* good ship *Mary-Joan*—in resplendent satisfaction, counting coins in a little chest, which was exactly like the pictures she'd always seen of pirate's booty—except for the size. The ship and this darling little coffer had just been liberated from a trader who had very little English, but who'd made his resentment very clear regardless...until she decided to let her boys play their favorite game: plank-walking.

She didn't let them do it with *every* ship they overcame: it would get tedious and uninteresting. But nothing cheered her crew like a Proper Piratical Walking The Plank. She'd not just read descriptions of it, but one of the pirate books she'd read in her youth had an illustration of a bound victim being forced by thrusting sabers held by evilly-grinning buccaneers down the inexorably uni-directional walk.

Now that she had seen the real thing, her own buccaneers grinned just as evilly as that picture. And it was actually a charitable choice—if you could swim. It gave the plank-walker a better chance of surviving their encounter with the Charlton Street Gang—now supplemented with a few sailors who understood how to make ships go, but who were too debauched to be chosen by any prudent ship's captain—as, if you stayed onboard, her boys were likely to get overexcitable and see any movement as a reason to "stab first and ask questions later."

This little chest was full of coins, most of them funny foreign things, but all of them glistening, glimmering gold and silver. She dug her fingers in and listened to the beautiful sound as they clinked musically back down onto the hoard.

She remembered the former captain again. He really had been an odd fellow. He had sworn at them in his foreign tongue, but his anger seemed feigned, and she'd had the strangest feeling he was *laughing* at her and her boys under his pretense of emotions he *should* have been feeling.

That feeling of inappropriate humor had increased dramatically when her boys made him walk the plank. *Made him*—it was more like he had egged them on. The more they shouted and prodded him with their weapons, the more he smirked.

He'd turned and saluted her before he stepped off the edge of the plank and dropped out of sight. The crew had cheered…but had she ever heard the splash?

Now they had confiscated his ship (their biggest one yet—an impressive two-masted one with ten guns, which she'd been told was called a "snow") and were doing a cruise of the New York/New Jersey Bight and her boys were arguing about keeping this one or selling it for a good price, because it was too conspicuous. She let them argue, while the gold coins spilled between her fingers. She *should* make them sell it, but it sailed so smoothly over the choppy waters, it was tempting to think of tricking it out as her piratical Ship of the Line…

"She is a darling ship, is she not? You are thinking how well she would look with a Jolly Roger on the mast? It would not be the first time she was thus bedecked…" The voice low in her ear (the ear she had left) was the same as the foreign captain and yet entirely different, as it was now an octave higher and with a British accent.

"Surprised to see me? I'm afraid I just *had* to play along with your little drama. In all the time I've been a pirate, I'd never actually seen *anyone* walk the plank."

Sadie turned her head slowly, a combination of shock and fascination washing through her. The person beside her still looked like the funny little ship's captain, very European and bearded. But then the beard was pulled away, and in an instant it was a female face, very pale and smooth, the lips thin but well-shaped, and the eyes the same mischievous hazel, although now their almond shape and long lashes looked very different in their altered frame.

"Ooooh, the look on your face!" the transformed captain cooed, pleased with Sadie's astonishment. "But why are you so surprised, little piratess? You know how difficult it can be to be a woman in a man's world. Not all of us can be a pirate queen in the open.”

“Wha—? Pirate queen? *You?*” Sadie felt like her brains couldn't catch up. She was making a fool of herself in front of this astonishing woman, but everything was moving too fast.

“Apologies for the irregularity of these introductions. I am Lady Ankaret Isobel L'Estrange Ruthven—” pronouncing the surname “Rivven”—the lady-captain stepped backwards to sweep a dramatic bow and flourish, “and you have pirated my vessel, the *Mary-Joan*. Although since *she* is sometimes the ship doing the pirating: you have made her thusly a *double* pirate ship.”

“I—do not understand. If you are pirates, why'd you let us board you? Why'd you let us think we'd gotten away with it?”

“You were having too much fun for me to stop you. So much enthusiasm! Your lads really *do* have that swashbuckler spirit, don't they?"

"But? You let us kill your crew!"

"My crew? Oh, they're not dead—although your lads gave them a good workout. They had a lark jumping off your plank, all scared and begging for their lives…and then they had a bit of a swim—and let me say, more than one of them needed a bath, so I must thank you—after which they climbed back up the sides of the ship. They are all belowdecks now, changing into dry clothes and having a drink and quiet laugh."

Sadie couldn't decide how to feel. On the one hand, she admired this woman immediately and wanted to ask her a million questions. On the other, this felt a bit too much like when Gallus Mag had so easily defeated her with that same unworried ease. She didn't like losing, and even less when it caused so little fuss for her opponent. She decided to focus on her admiration, at least for the time being, because she did very much want to learn what this Lady Ruthven knew about pirating.

Lady Ruthven smiled at her, and if it was a rather smug look, well, those who held the upper hand got to be that way. "Let's adjourn to my cabin. We can compare our life stories. I'm certain that yours will be fascinating!"

Sadie couldn't imagine how a Real Lady—and a Pirate Queen to boot—could find *her* life in anyway interesting, but Lady Ruthven was honestly attentive, riveted by her early life in New Orleans, asking many thoughtful questions. And she was even more engrossed by how Sadie came by her nickname, and the fight with Gallus Mag, and the months of riverine pirate life ever since.

But that was *after* Sadie had explained to her boys that they'd accidentally boarded a pirate ship, and after Lady Ruthven's crew had been called up to the deck. There were a few tense moments, but after Captain Ruthven, back in his seaman's beard, had saluted the Charlton Street Gang for their courage and fighting skills—and a cask of rum had been opened to celebrate—her boys had accepted the strange developments with good grace. They were now swilling grog with the *Mary-Joan*'s crew, telling tall tales of their exploits and singing sea shanties. The galley had resumed business, and Sadie and Lady Ruthven were seated at the captain's table, eating mutton and ham and fresh-caught mackerel and drinking a wine whose name Sadie pretended to recognize when Lady Ruthven had made a fuss presenting it.

Although, Sadie noticed, the Lady did not drink any of the fancy wine herself. Nor had she done more than move the food around her pewter plate. Sadie wondered if it were acceptable manners to offer to finish the plate for her...?

After Sadie finished her life's tale, Lady Ruthven took over with dramatic flourish.

"Ah, well, the Ruthvens have been titled since the 1600s. But there are too many of us knocking about the place—we have all the heirs we need and then spares upon spares. Us spares can either lounge about the family estates being pretty useless—especially if you are female and thus only ever going to be married off to some lord who will improve the family's wealth or prominence—or you can head into Town and have some fun and become a scandal and blacken your family's name. I did *that* for a bit, but it became tedious. It's just the same scandals over and over again, yawn." She both said "yawn" and yawned as she said it to demonstrate just how tiresome it all was. Sadie took note to steal that for future use.

Lady Ruthven continued, "Some far more thrillingly scandalous tales reached London, how some men of noble birth had become privateers, spending their lives fighting and wenching amongst the most villainous of scoundrels. That sounded better to me than wearing corsets and yards of skirts and needing smelling salts and spending the day resting on the fainting couch. I had always been considered a bit too *mannish*—although I think not a patch on your Gallus Mag!—so why not take the next step and *become* a man?

"I liberated some family heirlooms, and converted them into a ship—this ship, my sweet *Mary-Joan*—and some men's clothing suitable for a captain, and then found some men who were so desperate to leave their problems on the land that they were willing to crew for a green and rather effeminate captain like myself.

"I am now aware they'd planned to mutiny as soon as we were well out to sea…but before that could happen, my life took a far stranger turn. I ran into one cousin, who had run off for a more interesting and disreputable life years before: indeed, a bit of an inspiration to me. But he was entirely unlike the Cousin George I remembered. He was far stronger and more imposing. Life at sea had caused *quite* the sea-change. But…it was more than just sea air and the authority of command that had turned Cousin George into so puissant a man.

Lady Ruthven leaned towards Sadie, as if preparing to tell her the most intimate secret. Sadie leaned to meet her in response. She felt her heart racing, although she couldn't imagine what sort of secret could be more exciting than being a pirate in the first place.

"Georgie had become *more* than just a man. He had met a *creature* on his travels, one who walked and talked like a man, but who went out only at night, for he could not stand the light of the sun. This creature did not eat food nor drink wine...he lived entirely on the blood he drank from men and women!"

Lady Ruthven was growing excited as she spoke about this horror; her hazel eyes flashed with multicolored sparks in their depths, and her breath came faster, making her bosom rise and fall distractingly under the masculine-cut shirt. Sadie felt a corresponding thrill and goosepimples rose on her arms and the back of her neck.

"There have been penny-dreadfuls about such creatures, calling them 'vampires' or 'vampyrs,' but their real name is 'am'r,' and they are not only walking upon this earth, but they have been around for as long as any people have been. They hide amongst us, or they hide in secret fortresses away in the mountains or other lonely places, away from the commotion and bustle of mankind.

"But I am not like *them*," Lady Ruthven declared with sudden challenge in her voice, "I like noise and the busy-ness of living people—we call them, "kee." It is like being a hunter and living amongst your prey." And she stopped abruptly and stared at Sadie, daring her to answer.

Sadie knew she had to think real quick, and whatever she said next, it had better be *right*. But then again, that was not so hard, after all: in an instant, she understood that all her life she had pushed away fear and the conventions of normalcy and reached for the sublime and the *new*. And all this was *new* enough, alright.

"You're an *am'r*, ain't you?" She whispered, adrenaline whizzing through her as she spoke the impossible words. "He made you one of them, didn't he?"

"You're quick, for a kee," Lady Ruthven cooed, and laughed with a very lady-like trill. Sadie was very impressed with how she could one minute be so obviously a man, and the next so feminine you'd think it impossible she could ever be anything else. Was it on account of being an inhuman *creature*, that she could so easily break the bounds of sex?

"Yes, my bright girl, I am now an am'r too. For the minute I found out Cousin Georgie's secret, I demanded that he share his new powers: physical strength, compulsion over men and women, and the promise of eternal life and youth. I would have them for myself, and nothing he could say would dissuade me. For wasn't that just what I needed? If I was to be a successful pirate and captain of my own ship, I needed that compulsion. I needed that strength to impress my men in battle, to repulse any mutiny.

"And, oh, Georgie and I had *such fun* making me am'r just like him." Lady Ruthven's pale skin flushed, and her eyes were even brighter as she remembered whatever she was remembering. Sadie watched it all, wondering what might comprise those memories.

"I'm so jealous of ya," she confided to Lady Ruthven. "I want all that power and strength too!"

"And being young forever isn't so terrible, either," the Lady grinned at her, and Sadie was suddenly aware of how very *toothy* that grin was. "I am over a century old now—"she paused, to let Sadie look appropriately a-stonished. "And if Georgie hadn't made me am'r, I'd have gotten matronly and old before I died, and that would have been the most tiresome thing of all. Now I am free to forever fight and fuck and climb the rigging or swim in the moonlit seas."

"Oh!" Sadie couldn't help but sigh. "That's what I want, more'n anything else!"

"Is it, my little piratess…? I must admit, when I look at you, I see a good deal of my-self. Despite the disparity of our upbring-ings, we have fought the world to end up at sea, ruling over men and taking goods and even lives away from other men. Like me, you refused to be contained and constrained by your sex. I do admire that in a fellow woman…"

She narrowed her hazel eyes, looking Sadie up and down. Sadie shivered under the penetrating nature of it, as if Lady Ruthven could see all the way into her soul.

Lady Ruthven slammed her hand down on the table. "Why shouldn't you be am'r too, after all? There should be more of our sort of women in this world. Why not give you such power as well?"

"Oh!" Sadie was at first delighted, but then she wondered: *how does one become an am'r, after all?* Her trepidation was justified, because Lady Ruthven abruptly switched moods. "Although I will *not* tolerate ingratitude. If I make you am'r, you will recognize me as your 'patar,' your maker, and you will give me the respect and obedience that title deserves. If we both fight on these seas, you will never oppose me, but always engage in battle on my behalf, if I require you. Do you understand? Swear it to me!"

Sadie was leaning back so far her chair nearly toppled rearwards under the intensity of Lady Ruthven's insistence. But she took a deep breath and answered as calmly as she could, "Of course I understand, my Lady. I understand what an honor you're offering me, and I'd never disrespect you in any way. I'd always be mindful of what you'd done for me. I ain't likely to forget something like *that!*"

The Lady was somewhat mollified. "You'd be amazed what people can forget after only a few decades. But come, we understand each other. And after I do 'vhoon-vayon' with you—that's how I will make you an am'r like me—you'll find yourself much more *bonded* to my way of thinking."

Sadie wasn't too keen on whatever *that* meant, but it was too late to get out of it now. And, no doubt, she'd do whatever it took to get that promised strength and power. She'd figure out what to do about

Lady Ankaret Isobel L'Estrange Ruthven after that.

To her complete and utter surprise, the Lady pulled Sadie out of her chair and onto her lap. And then she put her arms around her and kissed her: a deep and passionate kiss, no hesitation or pause.

When, later, the Lady sunk her teeth deep into Sadie's neck as her fingers were gliding knowingly and equally unhesitatingly between Sadie's lower lips, it came as less of a surprise to Sadie than the kiss had been.

The Charlton Street Gang disappeared from the news for a long while after that. The Mayor and Police Commissioner took the credit, but the fly-cops of the East River waterfront shook their heads. They knew there was something funny about it, and while it was good riddance sure enough, they felt no assurance the Charlton Street Gang wouldn't be back.

Lady Ruthven invited Sadie's actual few seamen to join her crew, and Big Bill, Razor Charley, Saul, Slipsy, Piggy, Suds, Tommy, Patsy, Pete, Scotchy, and Wreck were taught true sailing by the salt-and-sun weathered veteran hands of the *Mary-Joan*. Meanwhile, Sadie learned about being an am'r-nafsh, which was not fully am'r, but no longer a normal human. She figured out quickly that she would need to avoid the suddenly cruel light of the sun. This was not very dismaying to her, as her existence had practically been nocturnal already; her only use for the sunlight hours had been for pickpocketing the honest folk of the daytime, and the occasional cruise of the Hudson with the afternoon sun warm on the Jolly Roger high on the *Lucky Lish*'s mast.

Sadie also learned the funny am'r language, which had words for all the new concepts Lady Ruthven was passing down to her. "Vhoon-vayon" was good; that was when she and the Lady gave each other pleasure with fingers and tongue and with blood—that was the "vhoon" part—often through the many long hours of the day.

The Lady would sometimes call in a member of the crew to the Captain's cabin. She would mesmerize him and then drink his vhoon-kee while Sadie would fuck him as the Lady directed. This didn't bother Sadie overmuch, but that was only because she would get to taste the Lady's vhoon-am'r, which made her more high than any knock-me-down liquor, hashish, or cocaine. Once she was flying in those rarified airs, whatever her body did was fine by her.

However, it was a reminder that the Lady not only saw herself as Sadie's social superior, but now there was the imbalance of the Lady being Sadie's "patar," the one who made her into an am'r, and Sadie was the lowly "frithaputhra," which Lady Ruthven said meant, "beloved child," but which in practice seemed to mean about the same as a glorified servant.

Sadie hadn't left her life in New Orleans to be subservient to *anyone*, not even an am'r. But she still had a lot to learn from Lady Ruthven. That mesmerism skill, for one. No man leaving the captain's cabin remembered what had actually taken place. They thought they had discussed celestial navigation or the condition of the ship's hull, or how much grog or salt pork or ship's biscuit needed to be obtained.

As it was, the men knew that "Cap'n Rivven" was "a bit funny," but it was blamed on his noble birth and upbringing. Every man aboard had no doubt that the Captain could grab him by the neck and dangle him overboard—hadn't they seen the Captain do it before? There was some question as to whether the Captain, who was on the shorter side, could do so with Big Bill, who towered more than a foot over the Captain's bicorn hat. Big Bill himself had no desire to put the matter to the question; he was entirely pleased with the pirate life at sea, and never wanted to set foot onshore again, at least not in any country where slavery was still the law of the land, or where folks acted like it still was.

Sadie dropped from the rope into a space on the deck that didn't have anyone currently fighting in it. Lady Ruthven and her most experienced fighters had been the vanguard swinging across onto the merchantman they had surprised in an early morning fog. Sadie was in the second wave. Her am'r-nafsh blood was throbbing with excitement, rushing throughout her body like it was pure alcohol; not that she could get drunk anymore. Blood and the increased capacity for violence were her booze now. Being even just halfway to being an am'r *and* being a pirate were the best combination. She was stronger than she'd ever dreamed, and the Pirate's Code was hardly anything like having rules. In this moment she was the happiest she'd ever been in her life.

Sadie landed lightly on her feet and immediately swept her cutlass three hundred and sixty degrees, taking in all the action around her, seeing if there was immediate danger from any direction, and, if not, where she should head first to join in the fun.

The fun was coming towards her, in the form of a huge sailor, knotted with muscle and scar tissue. He was twice her height and had a livid mark running from the twisted side of his mouth up to where he was missing an ear, which he probably assumed made him intimidating. If she'd still been a kee, Sadie definitely would have agreed. Now she just laughed with pleasure; he would be enough of a challenge to get the fight off to a good start.

One-Ear grinned as he charged her, as fast as he could while dodging other fights. He clearly thought that this would be a piece of cake. She'd be delighted to disappoint him.

He started with big slashes meant to rip through her defense or at least just scare her. She parried easily, holding eye contact to rattle him a bit. He'd expected her to be in pieces after the first slash of his heavy hacking-cutlass and his eyes went wide as she easily parried blow after blow with her smaller back-sword cutlass.

She'd been backing up a little as she met his strokes. It wasn't *entirely* pretense: he was very strong and moved his huge body with the rolling litheness you'd expect of a sailor. She didn't have Lady Ruthven's full am'r strength, not yet. She still had to take advantage of her street smarts and anything else she could turn to her advantage.

One-Ear was getting frustrated that he hadn't already cut this irritating petite brigand to bits. He judged his moment, and lunged for her chest with a momentum he felt would be unstoppable. He was right, in his way, except that he didn't expect her to step to the left and knock his sword aside, then follow that movement with a slash to his thigh.

It didn't incapacitate him, although if the fight lasted much longer it would slow him down. But now One-Ear was mad and not planning to let this fight last much longer.

This was fine with Sadie.

One-Ear, no longer grinning, lunged in at maximum momentum again, which was apparently a move which had never failed him before. She neatly stepped to her left and brought her own blade over his, sweeping his down to stick the tip in the deck. She kept applying pressure. Dismay and confusion moved through his face and body; she should not be able to keep his sword down like that!

Before he could recover, she yanked up her leg and kicked him in his bulky side with all the force she could bring. As he landed on the deck, winded and shocked, she bounced up in the air and landed, bringing her sword down into his chest, missing the heart but plunging deep into the lung. She made up for the miss by twisting the cutlass viciously left-right-left-right, and with a gush of bubbling blood from his mouth, he conveniently died.

Sadie stepped back and spun around again, looking for the next bit of fun. She was a little winded, so she breathed carefully, as she had learned she needed to do when practicing with Lady Ruthven. A sailor saw what she'd done to their crewmate and called to another mate to join him in avenging his death. This other sailor had been fighting Piggy, who was having almost as much fun as Sadie was. Piggy saw Sadie waiting and ducked a slash of Number Two's Spanish spadroon, then turned to engage another oncoming combatant. Sadie thought how kind of him it was to let her have this extra bit of play—and also deeply satisfying that the men of her crew so respected her fighting abilities.

But there was no time to think, only act, as Number One and Number Two came at her. The first was dead ahead of her, the second to her right, and both were trying to be the first to avenge the man she now had to be aware of as a large lump on the deck behind her.

At first, she acted purely defensively, blocking each thrust and cut, and taking baby steps back so that she could avoid the tripping hazard of One-Ear's lifeless lump.

She took their measure. They were experienced with fighting onboard a ship but had not trained to work together.

She let herself have some fun, parrying each attack by slapping the sword from Number One into Number Two and vice-versa. This slowed each fighter down, frustrating and confusing them. How satisfying it was to be frustrating and confusing men who'd underestimated her!

When this grew old, she deliberately turned all her apparent focus to Number One and "let" herself be maneuvered in between them. Number Two was glad to finally get the advantage of this infuriating little nuisance and lunged in to put an end to this bullshit.

As his spadroon sliced towards her, Sadie pivoted neatly on her hindfoot, and the blade sliced past her and deep into Number One. While Number Two tried to tug his sword from Number One's stomach he was trapped in a bent position, just *perfect* for Sadie to swing her cutlass up and take his head off. Well, her blade only went halfway through his neck, but that was really good enough for her. At least while she was still not a *full* am'r...

It hadn't taken long to subdue that merchantman. The *Mary-Joan* left a portion of her crew to sail the prize to Tortuga, where they would get the best price for the goods she carried and for the ship itself.

Lady Ruthven was very excited by the action, as usual, and although already replete with vhoon, had taken Sadie with her to the cabin to "question" the former captain and first mate of the merchantman, who of course had not survived the "questioning." Sadie had performed sexually as part of the process, getting plenty of Lady Ruthven's vhoon as payment. Sadie could manage to find it enjoyable in the moment, once the vhoon-am'r kicked in, but she was deeply weary of doing anything that anyone ordered her to do.

Sadie's reckless enthusiasm in fighting was not just a leftover from when she had been Sadie the Goat, but it was likewise informed by the fact that Lady Ruthven had explained that once Sadie died as a kee, she would rise again as a full am'r, far stronger and faster and quicker healing from even the most extreme injuries. And, most importantly, she'd be beyond the power of any other living being, kee or am'r. She'd be her own woman, fully able to set her own course in life and then allow nothing to get in her way. *Finally.*

Sadie didn't need to do anything much about the problem, she figured. A pirate's life was dangerous and unforgiving to the clumsy, the stupid, or the careless. All she had to do was fight a bit beyond her skills and strength, not restrain her tendencies to overestimate her abilities, and the "vis-tarascha," as Lady Ruthven called it, the death of her mortality, would take care of itself.

Sadie bided her time and absorbed as much as she could. Lady Ruthven was worldly; no one and nothing were above her cynical observations. Sadie memorized her opinions and mannerisms, the better to demonstrate her superiority when she returned home. For there was no doubt in her mind she would eventually return to New York City. She had unfinished business there.

Sadie strutted down Water Street.

Everything looked so different, but in a completely dissimilar way than when she'd first come to New York. That old Sadie was so scared, so small. She was, in fact, just like a little she-goat. She laughed out loud, remembering how she'd counted on surprising men simply by head-butting them. How trifling and pathetic that seemed. No wonder Gallus Mag had bested her so easily. Her laughter held sadness for The Sadie She'd Been.

The Sadie She Was Now moved through the nighttime streets not with a fake confidence bolstered by booze, but with the easy stride of a predator who knew she was the apex of her environment. There was no kee here who could hurt her. And while she could recognize any other am'r by scent—and there were some in the City—they were not here, in the fetid, filthy, dear old Fourth Ward.

Eyes followed her. No one called out, "Hey, Sadie tha Goat!" She had not changed in face or form, but her hairstyle was one she'd picked up from the local women on an island no one in the Fourth Ward had ever heard of. She wore a worsted wool walking dress, cream-colored and trimmed in navy like a sailor suit: all buttons and piping and neckerchief. It had been cus-tom-made for her by a tailor in Kingston. The skirt was easily torn off to reveal light-weight but durable drawers, in case fighting should break out. Sadie might no longer be a little she-goat, but the level of violence in her life had not noticeably decreased.

Here was the corner with Dover Street, and here was the Hole-in-the-Wall. She didn't see Gallus Mag's looming form on either side of the door, and she was starting to worry that perhaps she had lost her arch-enemy to disease or—even more likely—a knife in the back, but then Gallus Mag came up from the alley where she'd stepped away to piss. Relief washed through Sadie.

"Hey, ya slubber!" she called out, before Mag'd had the chance to recognize the on-coming female form, "Is there a drink in this shithole for me?"

"Why, as I live and breathe! Is it yourself, Sadie the Goat?"

"I am Sadie...but more than just a goat, now."

"So I sees. But whatever ya may be now...yer still short an ear!"

"I ain't forgotten the one ya bit off me, Gallus Mag."

"And I ain't neither, Miz-Sadie-the-Whatever. I have it in the jar, still. Safe and sound! It's the prettiest ear I ever got."

"I should hope so! Still...I'd like it back."

Gallus Mag leered hopefully at Sadie, "A rematch, is it? Ain't ya afraid of messing up that pretty dress? Or losing the *other* ear...?"

"Not particularly."

Mag wasn't an idiot. She could see Sadie's body language was completely relaxed. She wasn't drunk and bloviating. Indeed, Mag had never seen Sadie like this. And no one knew where Sadie had been in all this time. She was dressed and coiffured as if she now moved in an entirely different level of Society—which had not been a particularly likely fate for the old Sadie. This was both unexpected and incomprehensible. Mag had good reason to be cautious.

On the other hand, Sadie was still a delicate-looking little bloss. There she was, in all her feminine finery, looking no sturdier than she had the last time Mag had buttered her so easily. And Mag was always game, always more than ready to let loose her unquenchable rage.

Mag shot out a hand to grab Sadie's glamorous mass of braids, planning to bite the other ear off, as well. Sadie might hold herself different, but she was still nothing but a girleen, and even though she had foolishly come back for more, there was absolutely no way the little goat-girl could best Mag in a fight.

Mag's hand sank into the braids and started pulling Sadie's head over to the left—to add the right ear as well to the pickle jar—when Sadie's slender arm landed on Mag's and knocked the appendage away, an appendage which was suddenly limp and throbbing.

Mag was stunned in more than just her arm, for a moment. It felt like she'd been hit with a metal bar. How could Sadie have built up such force? And, after a strike like that, Sadie's arm should also feel a similar pain radiating out to shoulder and wrist as Mag's, but instead she was just standing in front of Mag, calm, with an annoying little smile.

Mag shook off the astonishment. It must be a freak chance; Sadie had accidentally hit her somewhere full of nerve endings. Mag transformed the pain into more rage, and with no warning, spun back towards Sadie's irritating smug mug with a full haymaker of a blow...

Only to feel her fist meet nothing but air, as Sadie leaned impossibly back and back, and Mag's arm shot over her backwards-curving body.

Sadie didn't waste the moment, but snapped her torso up, grabbed the extended arm, twisted with cruel strength, and torqued it up behind Mag's back, sending her stumbling head-first into the wall of the pub, the rotten wood of which shook under the impact.

Mag rolled to her back, both to protect it and to hold herself up so she did not drop to the mucky street. She panted one breath, but before she could properly fill her stunned lungs, Sadie had closed her face in to Mag's ear, and gave it a sharp little nip, like a cat. She breathed into Mag's now bloody ear, "I could have it off soooo easy. But I don't have a jar for it! And I don't want coves thinking I'm stealing yer trademark move. But yer slowing down, Mag—I'm disappointed. Is this the best ya got?"

A new wave of rage flowed through Mag from deep within, a raw, pure wrath that removed all confusion and dismay. She had twisted away from the sharp teeth and nasty, insinuating words, but that gave her room to bring her right elbow back a bit, ready to release it with a sudden unexpected momentum.

Mag drew in one sharp breath, then released her bent arm forward, a sharp blow to Sadie's liver that not even a corset would protect it from. It should leave the little bloss gasping and crying, back down in the filth of Water Street where she belonged.

But Sadie seemed almost to float backwards, and the punch landed with a disappointing soft sound. Sadie looked down, brushed imaginary dirt from her bodice, and looked back up to Mag with the same infuriating gentle smile.

The rage still flowed hot enough for Mag to overlook the unbelievable aspects of the fight. It was time to end this, whatever this fuckery was. Sadie had moved away to the perfect distance for the haymaker that had failed Mag before to finally have its desired effect. Mag struck without warning, shifting her weight and then her fist was rushing forward towards Sadie's face, planning to knock the maddening smirk off that pretty phiz. Sadie took a neat step to the side, and as Mag leaned forward into the unexpected void, Sadie shaped her hand like a knife and sliced it hard against the side of Mag's throat, the ever-so-vulnerable location being perfectly exposed. Mag dropped before her eyes had finished rolling back in her head.

Mag surfaced from the black pool of unconsciousness. She was down on the ground. She didn't remember anything after Sadie had done that funny thing to her neck... She blinked confusedly up from the filthy street at the dimber-mort who'd just so calmly taken down someone twice her size. Sadie was not showing any signs of exertion. No sweat beaded her brow, her chest did not rise and fall in double-time—nothing.

Mag's world abruptly rearranged itself. In her old reality, Sadie was an irritating little midge, barely worth the attention it took to squash her. Now, looking from the highly polished buttoned-up boots past the lustrous flounces of expensive fabric to the exotic hairstyle atop Sadie's head, Mag realized that Sadie was a being of strength and power, and more than that, she held both casually, without bother or haste.

Mag could not have put those thoughts into words: they were realizations in an unconscious part of her brain, but a part of her brain devoted to survival. She would not fight this reordering of the world: Sadie was now an equal, or more than an equal, and that was just how it was.

Mag sat up, rubbing her neck ruefully. "Well, *that* was a fancy trick. Will ya teach me?"

"Only if ya never use it on *me*," Sadie laughed, and gave Mag a hand up.

Their bodies coiled around and entangled with each other's, sinuous and effortless. They hardly had to learn one another; it was as if the years of enmity had somehow transformed to an innate understanding, and they knew almost before touching how a caress would satisfy the other.

Mag's decrepit rooms above the Hole-in-the-Wall had faded, with the rest of the world, to an unimportant background.

All that existed was their bodies and the mattress beneath them. It was only a rough wool blanket over a straw paillasse, but for this moment no finer luxury could be desired.

The first kisses had been rough, as rough as their fights, and both women tasted the iron tang of blood. Sadie had to hold herself back from biting harder for more, and she didn't mention that to Mag, not yet. Being am'r, while she could still technically enjoy the act without vhoon, tasting Mag's blood during the fight and now smelling Mag's blood under her skin was almost too distracting, and a part of her mind was set to the task of reminding her *not* to bite in every moment.

The next kisses were deeper, slower, and did not get in the way of undressing—at least Mag's clothes. Sadie's fancier rigging, aside from the rip-away skirt (which impressed the hell out of Mag), were more complicated things, and led to both women swearing between kisses as they tried to extricate Sadie from them.

After Sadie was finally as naked as Mag, mouths could find other places to explore, following fingers which discovered every inch of flesh, every in-curving and convexity, every smooth place and every patch of skin roughened by life, every scar honored with kisses.

The scars were gifted intimacies, and naturally after that, more intimacies could be risked, testing pressures and patterns for optimal pleasure: *Does she like this? Okay then how about this? No, not that, so maybe this?* But it had been so smooth, so easy, almost as if the violence they had shared before had prepared them for the sensuality: a physical understanding and an emotional depth neither of them expected.

Sadie found herself shocked by the joy she could feel, despite the lack of vhoon-vay-on. Playtime with Lady Ruthven had been fun at first, and then more just an act to be gotten through for the reward of the Lady's vhoon-am'r. But now, with no vhoon adding its intensity to the experience, Sadie found not only true physical pleasure, but an elation of spirit that she had never before felt without vhoon.

Sadie had never sought, nor expected to find love. But as she made Mag cry out in climax again and again, she wondered if maybe this was what it was.

And if so, what would love be like when vhoon was added to it...?

After the initial pleasuring, as Mag began to initiate Round Two, Sadie said, "Mag, go down and get yerself a beer—no I don't need one. But *you* will for what I'm about to tell ya."

So Mag brought up a foamy-headed pint and sat carefully on the bed with it, and listened as Sadie told her about the Charlton Street Gang boarding the *Mary-Joan* and the entirely unexpected Lady Ruthven, about becoming real, true pirates and sailing the Atlantic and the Caribbean and taking vessels and prisoners and booty, about stopping at Tortuga for watering and selling goods and prisoners, about breaming the *Mary-Joan* on a desert island and scraping the foulness off the bottom, about dancing with the crew on the deck through moonlit summer nights and pumping foul water from the bilges during a cyclone where she was sure they were all for certain going to Davy Jones' Locker. She told Mag about walking through towns in the West Indies and being treated with deference like she'd never dared hope for in this life, being fitted for fancy dresses at the same modistes as the governors' wives, waltzing the night away in fancy ballrooms.

"And you says this Lady Rivven can do all this fightin' and dancin' because she's 'ammer'?"

"*Am'r*. Yes...and the reason I can now do it all too is because I'm also am'r."

"And that's how yuh knocked me down on me arse, because yer stronger 'n any man?"

"Yes, though I've done some *learnin'* how to fight, as well. But no living man can best me now."

"I...*want* that. Sadie, my lovely Sadie, please—" Mag's voice caught against desperate longing in her throat. "Please would ya help me be an am'r, too...?"

"I was just hoping to hear ya ask, Gallus Mag. But it will cost ya two things: yer blood...and my ear."

Mag was frozen a moment. Then she laughed, deep spasms through her whole body. "Why Sadie, ya do never fail to knock me right over! The ear's yers, of course. But tell me 'bout the blood..."

"Let me *show* ya 'bout the blood..."

She showed her all the best ways that am'r and kee can exchange blood all that night. And the next. And the next.

"Come on, Mag, ya'll make us miss the tide!"

"By Jaysus and Mary, I dunno know how ya blarneyed me into this daftness."

"Here's the gang-plank, careful how you step—no, not there! There, I've got you. No falling in today."

"I could just stay 'n mind the bar. Sure I *don't* know I'm cut out to be a pirate..."

"You have violence in your heart and will do anything to survive. Mag, my love, you're born to rule the high seas with me. We'll have you swinging in the rigging in no time."

Mag looked dubiously at the sailors moving nimbly up masts and setting the sails to get underway. Suds waved down at Sadie, "Heya Captain Sadie! What's a-doin', Gallus Mag!"

"Suds...?" Mags could hardly tell him from the gangly, pimply lad who had lurched hopefully around the Fourth Ward, telling anyone who'd listen he'd be an arch-gonnoff someday. Seeing him sunburnt nut-brown and filled out with unlikely muscles, with a scar that ran from chin up his cheek to leave a groove in his long hair pulled back in a sailor's queue, Mag figured he'd fulfilled all his dreams.

If someone like *Suds* could thrive on this misbegotten vessel, which reminded her all too much of the ship which had brought her from Cork to New York...but wait! There were Slipsy and Scotchy climbing about like monkeys in the fragile-looking ropes, and Big Bill was up there on the quarterdeck, and if all those looby ralphs could make it in the pirate's life, well Gallus Mag sure as anything could too.

Sadie came back, and smiling from ear to ear, asked, "Wha' d'ya think of her?" Mag eventually guessed she was talking about the ship, and she still was pretty dubious about *that*, but she knew what she thought about Sadie, and that was good enough. She reached out and flicked the glass-fronted locket on Sadie's bosom, which encased a perfect shell-like ear.

"I think it looks better here than on your head," she grinned, an oft-repeated-joke.

"I think it was worth coming back t' get it," Sadie made the customary response. She added, "But it's time for us to leave the fuckin' Fourth Ward behind. It's too small for ya now. Am'r like us need the whole world. And the only way to get it is to sail the seas."

"Well...mayhap it'll be better as an am'r," Mag grumbled.

"And as a guest of the captain! Until we find what job yer best suited for."

"Can I be the bouncer at the captain's door?"

"You know I don't need that...but ya can be the first to cross over to our prizes and subdue any who'd try to fight."

"That...don't sound half bad." Mag brightened.

"Ya'll love it. The sudden rush of brutality. An' all the blood..."

"All the blood I can drink—ya promised that!"

"That will not be a hard promise to keep. And ya can start a new ear jar, if ya like." Sadie smiled, and tossed her head, making the ear-locket quiver where it rested between her breasts.

"Or I could wear 'em as a necklace like you do!"

"Anything you like, Magnificent Mag. There are no rules out here, not for the likes of you an' me."

"Ya said there's a Pirates' Code."

Sadie grinned hugely. "It's more of a *guideline*. There's nothing holding either of us down, not ever again."

"Then I love this life already, m' Pirate Queen."

"Look! See how far we are from land already? Welcome to yer kingdom, yer Majesty."

Sadie the Goat and Gallus Mag will return in *Blood Depths*, Book IV in the Blood & Ancient Scrolls Series

Indie authors need reviews to survive. Amazon treats us better the more reviews our books have. So please, if you enjoyed this story. take a moment to review it here:

https://www.amazon.com/review/create-review/?ie=UTF8&channel=glance-detail&asin=BOFG4GNN9Z

Thank you so much for your time—you are very appreciated!

Index of Selected Items from The Rogue's Lexicon

ackruffs: river-thieves; river-pirates

arch-gonnoff: the chief of a gang of thieves

ark: a ship; a boat; a vessel

bene: good; first rate

bens: fools

bleak-mort: a pretty girl

bloss: woman; mistress; girl

blowen: the mistress of a thief

bludget: a female thief who decoys her victims into alley-ways, or other dark places for the purpose of robbing them

blunderbuss: an ignorant, blustering fellow

bottle-head: stupid fellow

cap your lucky: run away

consolation: to kill a man is to give him consolation

cove: a man; a fellow

cramped: killed; murdered

cull: a man

dell: a prostitute

dimber-mort: pretty girl; enchanting girl.

fly-cop: sharp officer; an officer that is well posted; one who understands his business.

frog and toe: the city of New York

frumper: a sturdy blade

gob: the mouth

goosecap: a silly fellow; a fool

got him down fine: know for a certainty; know all his antecedents

hoody-doody: a short clump of a person

kinchin coves: boys taught how to steal

looby: an ignorant fellow; a fool.

mab: a harlot

mill: the treadmill; a fight

millingcove: a pugilist

mizzle: go; run; be off

moll: a woman

mort: a woman

mouthing: crying

na dann: a German phrase, commonly translates to "well then"

nockyboy: a simpleton

pike: to run away; to pike off

rag-water: intoxicating liquor of all kinds. (If frequently taken to excess, will reduce any person to rags.)

ralph: a fool

red rag: the tongue; "shut your pota-to-trap and give the red rag a holiday," "shut your mouth and let your tongue rest"

roughs: men that are ready to fight in any way or shape

sharp: a man that is well posted; one who "knows a thing or two;" a gambler

slubber: a heavy, stupid fellow

Verdammt!: German for "Damn it!"

From

VOCABULUM;

OR, THE ROGUE'S LEXICON.

COMPILED FROM THE MOST AUTHENTIC SOURCES.

BY GEORGE W. MATSELL, SPECIAL JUSTICE, CHIEF OF POLICE,

NEW-YORK:

1859

(Many thanks to Project Gutenberg, one of the most important resources on the internet)

Glossary of the Am'r Language

AM'R WORD • DEFINITION

adharmhem • one who endangers am'r as a whole, or the act of endangering the am'r as whole

ahstha • coma am'r fall into when deprived off too much blood and/or oxygen

am'r *(sing. & pl.)* • commonly known as a "vampire"

am'r-nafsh *(sing. & pl.)* • A living human being who shared blood with an am'r three times, but not yet died.

Aojasc' am'ratv! • "Strength and immortality!"

aojysht *(sing.)*, **aojyshtaish** *(pl.)* • am'r elder, am'r elders

bakheb-vhoonho • giver of blood, used for am'r who give blood to other am'r or kee; used for the stronger blood going to the weaker, whether am'r or kee

cinyaa • my lover

esteshcinast • *verb:* to know by smell, specifically to recognize the vhoon-anghyaa of other am'r *(Present tense: "I esteshcinasti", past tense "I have esteshcinastii")*

fraheshteshnesh • first blood meal as a newly awoken am'r

frangkhilaat • to feed / take nutrition from a kee

frithaputhra *(sing.)*, **-ish** *(pl.)* • "beloved child", title used by a am'r for an am'r / am'r-nafsh made with the former's blood

gharpatar • grandfather, maker of my maker

izchha *(sing.)*, **-ish** *(pl.)*   •   a "sacrifice", a mortal who is selected to donate blood (with or without sex)

kee *(sing. & pl.)*   •   mortal, non-vampire, living human being

maadak   •   intoxicating drink; effects am'r like strong hallucinogen / tranquilizer

maadakyo   •   corrupted with maadak, a mortal who has drunk maadak

pat'rkosh   •   patar-killer

patar   •   "parent" or "maker"; title used by a am'r or am'r-nafsh for the am'r who made them

tokhmarenc   •   dying the final death; "giving the tokhmarenc" is killing another am'r so they cannot rise again

vhoon   •   blood

vhoon-anghyaa   •   blood influence, blood-line, the traits that come down from your patar; also the smell of your patar in your blood

vhoon-berefteh • to be bled

vhoon-vaa • am'r-style healing with blood

vhoon-vayon • am'r love making, with other am'r or am'r-nafsh

vistarascha • dying the mortal death; becoming am'r

Acknowledgements

First and foremost, I want to thank Lauren for both demanding that I write this and providing enthusiastic encouragement along the way. She is the one who demanded some shorter stories from me, and it has led to me doing some projects in the Blood & Ancients Scrolls series that have been deeply satisfying to me as a writer, and helped me move my craft forward. Everyone needs a friend who gets their ass into gear.

Thanks to Tiffany for her usual superior editing. I know I can count on her to make sure I don't miss something vital.

Thanks to Kevin Foster for a nautical edit-ing pass, to ensure that people who have saltwater in their veins don't wince when reading my best efforts to pretend I'm not a total lubber.

As always, thanks to Trent for help chore-ographing fight scenes. He always takes the time to find out what the characters are like, what their emotional states are, and what location and weapons and all other factors are, and then helps me work through how the fights flow. If you think I write good fight scenes, it's mostly because of him.

Everything I got right in the first draft of this, before the aforementioned help came along, is a huge debt I owe to Patrick O'Bri-an. I have circumnavigated the Aubreyad enough times that I have honestly lost count. O'Brian has deeply impacted my writing (and my tendency to yell "Wittles is up!" at dinnertime) and I honestly wouldn't have dared to take on even a partial ship-board adventure without that little splash of seawater in my soul.

Finally, as always, thanks to my readers. They are the ones who, when I couldn't come up with a title for this and was using the working title of "That Lesbian Vampire Pirate Story" said to me, "Why not just go with that? It works for us!" So I listened to them, because they know best.

About Raven Belasco

Raven Belasco's writing style has been described as both "darkly lyrical" and at the same time "an easy, breezy writing style; a more colloquial and relaxed John Scalzi." A degree in Comparative literature and a lifetime devotion to genre fiction fused into her unique style: constructed with the same dedication as literary fiction, yet easily accessible for any reader.

Belasco wanted to be an author since she was a little eight-year-old bookworm. When she turned seventeen she became chronically ill, and reading and writing "saved" her. After college, she had success with many published articles and short stories, but she always wanted more. Her first novel, *Blood Ex Libris*, was a genre-blending mix of dark fantasy, horror, historical, and action-adventure. It turned out to be very hard to get an agent to consider that, and it was only through dedication and a stubborn refusal to quit that Belasco finally found a publisher who understood her fresh voice and message.

To keep up with the Blood & Ancient Scrolls series, you can sign up for Raven's Newsletter at

https://ancientscrolls.beehiiv.com

Or find her online: https://ravenbelas.co/